Amy Animal Talker

The Star-Struck Parrot

Diana Kimpton

Illustrated by
Desideria Guicciardini

USBORNE

The Clamerkin Clan

Hilton

Amy

Einstein

Plato

Isambard

Willow

Bun

To Helena

First published in the UK in 2010 by Usborne Publishing Ltd., Usborne House, 83-85 Saffron Hill, London EC1N 8RT, England. www.usborne.com

Text copyright © Diana Kimpton, 2010

Illustrations copyright © Usborne Publishing Ltd., 2010

The right of Diana Kimpton to be identified as the author of this work has been asserted by her in accordance with the Copyright, Designs and Patents Act, 1988.

Cover photograph © Getty Images/Dave King

The name Usborne and the devices ♀ ♛ are Trade Marks of Usborne Publishing Ltd.

A CIP catalogue record for this book is available from the British Library.

First published in America in 2013 AE.

PB ISBN 9780794533878   ALB ISBN 9781601303110

JFMA JJASOND/13   02363/1

Printed in Dongguan, Guangdong, China.

CHAPTER ONE

"Wow!" said Amy Wild as she walked down the field next to the Community Hall. On a normal day, she could see the sea from here. But today, her view was blocked by a cluster of huge tents. "Does it really take this many people to make a movie?"

"Of course it does," squawked Plato, the parrot, from his perch on her shoulder. "I've watched programs about it on TV."

Hilton, the cairn terrier, looked up from the tent peg he was sniffing. "I still don't understand why they've come. It would be easier to make the movie in their studio rather than drag everything all the way to Clamerkin Island."

Amy wasn't surprised to hear Hilton and Plato speaking. The string of glittering metal paws she wore around her neck was magic. It gave her the power to talk to animals.

She smiled at the dog and said, "I think they've come for the sea. They must need that, because the posters they put up said the movie's called *Sea Fever*."

"It's not just the sea," said Plato, proudly fluffing out his chest feathers. "The movie is set in the past, and the director said on TV that Clamerkin is the perfect place to film the harbor scenes. Apparently the Island is charmingly old-fashioned with picturesque buildings and cobbled streets. It's also delightfully quiet."

"It's not today!" said Amy, as they reached the bottom of the field. The harbor ahead of them was a hive of activity. Some people were setting up lights and cameras. Others were busy piling up barrels, crates and sacks to make the harbor look like a scene from history.

"I've never seen a boat like that," barked Hilton, as he pointed his nose at the three-masted schooner tied up by the dock.

"It's not a boat," squawked Plato, hopping from foot to foot in excitement. "It's a ship – a pirate ship. The movie must have pirates in it. And *that* means they're sure to need a parrot."

Amy reached up and stroked the parrot's head. "Don't get your hopes up too much. The ad for movie extras didn't say anything about animals."

"I expect they've brought a parrot with them," said Hilton. He gazed around at the equipment stacked in all directions. "They seem to have brought everything else."

"It doesn't matter if they have," said Plato. "I'll show them that I'm the best bird for the part." He flew onto a nearby fence and limped along the top of it, squawking, "Pieces of eight, pieces of eight. Yo ho ho and a bottle of rum."

Amy watched him with concern. "Have you hurt your foot?" she asked.

Plato sighed. "Of course I haven't. I'm pretending that I've got a wooden leg."

"I think it's the pirate that has that – not the parrot," barked Hilton.

"And I'm the only human who will understand what you're saying," said Amy. "Can't you do that pretend talking that some parrots learn?"

"No," said Plato. "All that Pretty Polly stuff never seemed worth the effort until now."

At that moment, a man strode along the dock talking into a megaphone. "Everyone who wants to be an extra come with me," he announced.

"That's us," said Amy. She stepped forward and followed the man to three tables set up at the far end of the harbor. So did a crowd of other people. Everyone on Clamerkin Island had seen the ads for extras, and nearly all of them wanted to be in the movie.

The man made them form a line in front of each table – one for the men, one for the women and the third for the children. Plato perched on a nearby ladder while Amy got in line. Her friend, Veronica, slipped into place behind her.

Amy smiled at her. "Isn't this exciting? It's a great way to spend school break."

"It's much better than lessons," Veronica agreed. "I wonder what happens next."

"I expect we wait," said Amy.
"Someone told me there's lots of
waiting around in filming." She
was careful not to mention that the
someone was Plato. Veronica didn't
know Amy could talk to animals.

Neither did any other human except Granty, her great-aunt. It was Granty who had given her the necklace and Granty who warned her to keep its powers secret.

The line moved faster than Amy expected. The people at the table dealt with everyone so quickly that it wasn't long before it was her turn.

"Hello. I'm Fran," said the lady who was dealing with the children. "Do you have your permission form?"

Amy pulled a piece of paper out of her pocket and handed it over. "My mom and dad have both signed it."

Fran read the form quickly and added Amy's name to her list. "Are they extras too? There needs to be someone around to keep an eye on you."

"They're doing the catering," Amy explained. "They've closed the Primrose Tea Room for the week so they can be down here making the food for the cast and crew."

"That's fine," said Fran. "Now walk over to that pile of boxes, turn around and walk back again. Don't try to act — just be yourself."

Amy found it hard to be herself when she knew she was being watched. First she worried that she was going too fast so she slowed down. Then she worried she was going too slowly so she speeded up. She was relieved when she finally got back to the table. But the waiting wasn't over yet.

Amy's mouth went dry with nerves as she watched Fran scribble some notes on her list. Had she passed the audition? Had she gotten a part?

At last, Fran finished writing and looked up. Then she smiled at Amy and said, "Great job. You can be Girl 5."

Amy was delighted. "Thanks," she said, with a big grin. "What do I have to do?"

"Pretty much what you just did," Fran explained. "You'll be walking around the dock, helping to make it look busy while the sailors load the ship." She paused while she wrote *Girl 5* beside Amy's name. Then she looked up and said, "Make sure you're here at 6:30 sharp tomorrow morning for wardrobe."

Amy's mouth dropped open with shock. "That's early."

"It always is in the movie business," Fran explained. Then she looked over Amy's shoulder and called, "Next!"

Veronica started to step forward,

but Amy didn't move out of her way. Instead she handed over another form and said, "This one's for my parrot. He doesn't have a mom or dad so I signed it for him."

Fran roared with laughter. "So you think your parrot wants to be in the movies."

"I'm sure he does," said Amy. "And he'd be a perfect parrot for a pirate."

Plato spotted his big moment and flew down onto the table. "Shiver me timbers," he shouted, as he fluffed out his feathers. "Ship ahoy, me hearties."

But Fran couldn't understand him. All she heard was some very loud squawking. She pushed Plato gently toward Amy and said, "I'm sorry. We don't need a parrot. There aren't any pirates in this story."

Plato's head drooped in disappointment. He had dreamed of being on screen like the stars he loved watching on TV. But now that chance was gone.

Amy stroked his feathers and lifted him back on to her shoulder. It seemed so unfair that she had a part, but he didn't. Surely there was some way she could help him be in the movie?

CHAPTER TWO

The food tent was already busy when Amy walked inside with Plato and Hilton. Mom and Dad were busy serving other people, but Granty wasn't. She brought Amy a glass of milk and a sandwich. Then she gave Plato a grape. "He does look sad," she said. "Have they turned him down?"

Amy nodded. "I don't think they

want any animals."

"They want hers," said Granty, pointing at a woman sitting at a table in a quiet corner of the tent. "She was telling me earlier that she's the official animal trainer for this movie. Why don't you talk to her?"

Amy carried her drink and plate to the same table and asked, "Is it all right if I sit here?"

"Of course it is," the animal trainer replied with a smile. Then she shook Amy's hand and added, "I'm Jane from Star Pets."

"I'm Amy from the Primrose Tea Rooms. And this is Plato and Hilton."

Amy was about to sit next to Jane when she realized the chair was

already taken. There was a small cage
on it — the sort of carrier designed for
taking cats to
the vet. But
there wasn't
a cat inside.
There was
a Yorkshire
terrier with long,
perfectly groomed hair.

The terrier growled at Amy.

"Bad boy," Jane scolded.

"Boy!" barked Hilton. "What's a
boy dog doing with a pink bow on his
head?"

Plato squawked with laughter. "He's
so small that he makes you look big."

Jane looked at them both and

sighed. "Your pets look a lot happier than mine." Then she put a finger through the cage's wire mesh and tried to tickle the dog's ears. "Please cheer up, Cuddles."

"Leave me alone," grumbled the terrier. He turned around on his velvet cushion and pointed his backside at his owner.

"Maybe he wants to get out," Amy suggested, as she sat down next to him. "It can't be much fun in there."

"But it is clean," said Jane. "We can't have the canine star of the movie getting his feet dirty."

Amy looked at the sulky terrier with new respect. "Is he really a star?" she asked.

"He's definitely the most important dog in the movie," Jane replied. Then she laughed and added, "But that's because he's the only one."

Suddenly her pager bleeped. "The director wants to talk to me," she said as she jumped up from her chair. She started to pick up the cage. Then she changed her mind. "I don't want him seeing Cuddles in this mood. Can I leave him here with you for a few minutes?"

Amy agreed willingly. There was no one else sitting near them so this would be an ideal opportunity to talk to the Yorkshire terrier without being noticed. She waited until Jane was out of sight. Then she tapped the side of the cage to attract the dog's attention.

"Get lost," snapped Cuddles.

Hilton put his front feet on the chair and glared at the terrier. "Mind your manners," he warned. "That's no way to speak to my human."

"Mind *your* own manners," squawked Plato. He flew onto the carrier and tapped Hilton on the nose with his beak. "That's no way to speak to an *actor*." Then he tipped his head to the side and looked at Cuddles. "You are an actor, aren't you?"

The Yorkshire terrier gave a huge sigh. "I suppose I am. But I wish I wasn't."

"Why?" asked Amy.

Cuddles opened his eyes wide with amazement. "Can you understand what we're saying?"

"Of course I can." She put her hand to her throat and held out the necklace of paws. "This is magic. It lets me talk to animals."

The dog moved as close to her as he could and peered at the necklace. "Fascinating," he said. "I've been in lots of movies with pretend magic. But I've never seen the real thing before."

Plato edged between them. "You still haven't explained why you wish you weren't an actor."

"It's so boring," said Cuddles. He opened his tiny mouth in a tiny yawn that revealed some equally tiny teeth. "I have to stay clean and wear sappy pink bows and be on my best behavior all the time. I'm not allowed to sniff around trees or dig holes or chase sticks."

"That's awful," said Hilton. "It's that sort of thing that makes it fun to be a dog."

"And then there's my name," grumbled the Yorkshire terrier. "What self-respecting dog wants to be called Cuddles?"

"What would you like instead?" asked Amy.

Cuddles wagged his tail. "Fang would be good. So would Scar or Gnasher."

Hilton started to howl with laughter.

But he stopped when Amy gave him a warning glance. "Shh!" she whispered. "You'll hurt his feelings and you'll attract attention."

"But those are names for fierce dogs," said Hilton. "The sort that have spikes on their collars."

"So?" said Cuddles. "I could have spikes too."

"Only very small ones," said Plato.

Their conversation was cut short by Jane's return. "Thanks for looking after him," she said. She picked up the cage, peered inside and smiled at Cuddles. He scowled back at her. Then she said, "See you again," and headed toward the tent door, carrying the cage in one hand.

"Has he put you off wanting to be in the movie?" Hilton asked Plato, as they watched the animal trainer and her dog walk away.

"Absolutely not," squawked the parrot. "I still want that more than anything else in the world."

Amy wished she could do something to help Plato. Then she looked at the cage swinging in Jane's hand and had an idea. "Let's go back to the Primrose," she said. "I need to look for something."

CHAPTER THREE

The attic of the Primrose Tea Room was divided into two. One half was Amy's bedroom. The other was a store full of clutter – things no one wanted anymore but couldn't bring themselves to throw away.

As soon as Amy got back, she ran up the stairs with Plato and Hilton. Then she pushed open the storeroom door, and stepped inside. It was dark and had the musty smell places get when they've been shut up for a long time.

She reached out and pressed the light switch. The single bulb hanging from the ceiling glimmered into action. It cast dark shadows among the jungle of objects, making them look scarier than they would by the light of day.

Plato gulped. "I think I'll wait for you outside," he announced. "It's a little crowded with all of us in here."

Hilton looked around nervously. "Will this take long?"

"No," said Amy. "I know what I'm looking for. I'm sure I saw it over in that corner when I was up here with Dad." She stepped over a pile of yellowing papers, wiggled past an old sofa and stopped at a table piled with dusty ornaments and old vases.

She peered under the table and gave a shout of triumph. "Here it is," she cried, as she pulled out a parrot cage. "Now we just need to hide it near the harbor ready for tomorrow."

*

The sun had just appeared over the horizon when Amy set off for the movie set the next morning. Hilton and Plato went with her. So did Mom, Dad and Granty, ready to cook breakfast for the crew.

When they reached the food tent, Amy waved goodbye and headed off in the direction of another tent labeled *Wardrobe*. As soon as she was sure her parents weren't watching, she slipped away to the path beside the Community Hall. The parrot cage was still where she had hidden it the evening before. She pulled it out of the bushes and opened the door.

Plato flew down and popped his

head inside. "Do I have to go in now?" he asked. "I'm not very good with small spaces."

"You can just sit on top for the moment," Amy replied. "But you must get inside as soon as you see me coming. Otherwise the plan won't work, and you won't be in the movie."

"I promise I will," said Plato, shivering with excitement. "This is my big chance. I'm not going to spoil it."

Amy left him there and ran back to the wardrobe tent. It was already thronging with people. Some were still in their own clothes. Others were already in costume, looking as if a time machine had brought them here from two centuries ago.

"Hello, Amy," said an old-fashioned sailor with a beard. "I'm helping to organize the children." He marked her name off on the clipboard he was carrying and added, "You're Girl 5. Go to the second cubicle on the right."

Amy peered through the whiskers stuck on the sailor's face and recognized her principal. "Thanks, Mr. Plimstone," she said, and ran off in the direction he was pointing.

Twenty minutes later, Amy looked in the mirror and hardly recognized herself. Her jeans and T-shirt had been replaced with a long dress with frilly pantaloons underneath. Her dark hair was partly hidden by a bonnet with fake ringlets attached, and her feet were wearing lace-up boots instead of her usual sneakers. Even her necklace wasn't visible. It was safely hidden under the dress's collar.

To her relief, the wardrobe lady didn't give her anything to carry. That was good. She needed her hands free to put her plan into action.

As she stepped out of the tent, Fran came over to tell her what to do. "In the scene we're filming, the ship is being loaded up ready for the voyage. You start over there by that pile of sacks. When the director shouts 'Action!', I want you to walk slowly across the dock toward the prow of the ship, looking at everything on the way. When he shouts 'cut', you stop. Is that clear?"

Amy nodded. "I think so." She stood by the sacks until Fran was busy with someone else. Then she ran off to the

path by the Community Hall. Plato
was still sitting on top of the cage. He
tilted his head to the side when he saw
her coming and asked, "Is that you?
You look very different."

"Of course it's me," she hissed. "Now
get inside."

Plato immediately did as he was told.
Amy slammed the door shut behind
him. Then she picked up the cage and
ran back to the movie set with it. By
the time she arrived, all the actors were
in position, ready to start the scene.

She took her place quickly, holding
the cage behind her where it couldn't
be seen by the cameras. She didn't
want anyone to notice it before the
scene started.

Suddenly, a grubby tabby cat jumped on to the pile of sacks beside her. He looked admiringly at the equipment cluttering up the dock.

"Wonderful things, cameras," he said. "Look at that one up there. It's on a sort of crane."

"Hello, Isambard," said Amy.

Before she had a chance to say any more, the director called "Action!" and all the actors started to move. Amy set off toward the ship on the route Fran had shown her. As she walked, she tried hard to look interested in everything that was happening around her. She also held up the parrot cage as high as she could so Plato was in full view of the cameras.

Plato sat up proudly. He was obviously enjoying every second of his moment of fame. Which was a good thing, because it didn't last long.

CHAPTER FOUR

"Cut!" shouted the director. He pointed at Amy and demanded, "What is that child carrying?"

A weasel-faced young man in a baseball cap ran over and peered into the cage. "It looks like a parrot," he announced.

"A parrot!" yelled the director. "I didn't ask for a parrot. The only bird in this movie is the *Black Raven*."

"That's not fair," squawked Plato. "What's a raven have that I don't?"

The young man didn't understand him. "Noisy thing, isn't he?" he said to Amy. "You'd better get rid of him quick."

Amy ran and put the cage behind the nearest camera, where Plato could see what was happening on set. She was careful to leave the door undone so he could get out if he wanted to.

She was about to run back to her place when the young man noticed Isambard. "Shall I get rid of this cat, too?" he asked. "There wasn't a cat on your list of props."

The director didn't reply right away.

Instead, he walked around the pile of sacks, examining Isambard from different directions. "No," he said eventually. "He can stay. He's just the right sort of cat for a place like this."

"That's not fair either," squawked Plato. "Why aren't I the right sort of parrot?"

"Shush!" said Amy. "You've got to keep quiet or they won't let you watch."

"I'm not sure I want to now," grumbled the parrot. He turned his back on the movie set and poked his head under one wing.

Amy left him there and ran back to her place. She only just reached it in time. "Action!" shouted the director again, and the second take was under way.

Amy was determined not to get into trouble again – she would never be able to help Plato get a part if she was thrown off the set. So she acted as hard as she could as she walked toward the ship.

It was the first time she had been really close to it. And it was the first

time she had noticed the words "Black Raven" painted on its side in gold letters. The sight of them made her smile. Perhaps Plato would feel happier when he heard there wasn't another bird in the movie after all.

When the first scene was finally finished, Amy and the other extras were allowed to have a break. "We don't need you for the next scene," Fran explained. "It's some close-ups of the heroine arriving on the dock."

Most of the others headed for the food tent. But Amy went to check on Plato. She was pleased to see that he'd gotten over his huff and was sitting beside Hilton, watching the filming. He perked up even more when she explained about the *Black Raven*.

"But it's still not fair about Isambard," he grumbled.

"What's wrong with him?" asked Hilton. "I thought he looked really good on those sacks."

"I don't care if he does," said Plato. "It's just not right – him being in the movie when I'm not."

A sudden commotion caught their attention. The star of the movie had arrived. Amy had seen Dallas Riba before on screen, but she was much more impressive in reality. She was playing a countess in love with the ship's captain, and she looked magnificent in her long dress and flower-trimmed hat.

"That costume suits you beautifully," said the director. "Now we just need your lapdog to add the finishing touch." He clapped his hands and called, "Bring the dog over here."

"Do they mean me?" asked Hilton.

"They'd better not," said Plato. "That

would be the last straw as far as I'm concerned."

"It's not you," said Amy. "It's Cuddles."

As they watched, Jane from Star Pets stepped forward, carrying Cuddles's cage. She put it down on a chair and lifted out the Yorkshire terrier. His long silky hair was smooth and glossy. His bow was tied perfectly on top of his head. But the dog looked even more miserable than he had the day before. His eyes were sad and his tail drooped.

Jane waited while Dallas took up her position in front of the cameras. Then she placed Cuddles in the star's arms, straightened his bow and carefully arranged his long hair.

The director waited until she had moved away. Then he shouted, "Action!"

As if on cue, Cuddles sank his tiny teeth into Dallas Riba's hand. The star screamed and tossed him away. Jane tried to catch him, but she wasn't quick enough. Cuddles landed on his feet and fled, dodging between people's legs and jumping over the cables that snaked across the ground.

Jane tried to run after him, but the director stopped her. "What's the meaning of this?" he bellowed. "I thought that dog was trained."

"So did I," Jane wailed. "I'm ever so sorry. He's never done that before."

"And he's not getting the chance to do it again," said the director. "We'll have to use a different lapdog."

Jane stared at him in dismay. "I don't have one."

"Then get one," ordered the director. He looked around and pointed at Hilton. "He'll do."

"No! No! No!" squawked Plato, jumping up and down on top of his cage. "It's not fair."

To the parrot's delight, Dallas killed Hilton's chance at fame before it had even started. "I'm not holding any more dogs," she announced, as she waved her hand in front of the director's face. "Look what that little horror did to me. I'd have been really hurt if I hadn't been wearing gloves."

"I know, darling," said the director in a soothing voice. "But you know you've got to hold a pet. It's in the script."

Dallas folded her arms and glared at him. "All right," she agreed. "But no dogs. You'll have to find me some other sort of animal."

Plato gave a whoop of delight. "This is my big chance," he squawked. "She needs a lap parrot." Before Amy could stop him, he flapped his wings and soared into the air. Then he dived down into Dallas Riba's arms.

CHAPTER FIVE

The movie star had obviously never met a lap parrot before. She beat at Plato's brightly colored feathers with her hands, trying to drive away what she thought was a crazy bird attacking her.

Amy ran toward her, shouting, "He's not trying to hurt you. He's just being friendly."

"I'd hate to see him when he's not," snapped Dallas. She grabbed the script from her assistant's hands and used it to lash out at the parrot.

Fortunately she missed. But Plato got the message. "There's no need to be unpleasant," he squawked, as he retreated to the top of his cage. "I was only trying to help."

The director watched him go. Then he turned his attention back to Dallas. "So dogs are out, and you don't seem too big on birds. Is there any kind of animal you would agree to hold?"

Dallas pursed her lips and thought for a moment. Then she smiled and said, "I like cats."

Jane shook her head. "I didn't bring a cat with me. You only asked for a dog."

"That's no excuse," snapped the director. "You're supposed to be an animal trainer. So find a cat and train it."

"Will that one do?" asked Jane, pointing at Isambard.

"Of course not!" snapped the director. "I've already filmed him so we can't use him twice." He took his script back from Dallas and waved it under Jane's nose. "It's vital to the story that the heroine is carrying a pet when she arrives. We're filming that scene this afternoon, so you've got until then to produce a cat. If you don't, that's the end of your movie career. I'll never use Star Pets again."

He turned and ushered Dallas away to work on a different scene. As soon as he had gone, Jane sat down on a chair and put her head in her hands. "I'll never do it," she groaned.

"Do you need some help?" asked Amy.

Jane looked up and gave a weak smile. "I think I need a miracle. I have no idea where to find another cat. And I've still got to find Cuddles." Her smile vanished, and her eyes filled with tears. "I hate to think of him lost and alone."

"I expect the other extras would help us look for him," said Amy. "And I know several cats on the Island. I can see if one of them wants to be in the movie."

Jane laughed. "That's a funny thing to say. You make them sound as if they think like people."

Amy forced herself to laugh, too. But she was worried by Jane's comment. Although she wanted to help the animal trainer, she must be careful how she did it. She mustn't give away the secret of the necklace.

Amy was right. All the extras were glad to have something to do while they were waiting around between scenes. By the time filming stopped for lunch, they had searched every possible hiding place on the harbor – some of them more than once. But there was no sign of Cuddles.

"I hope he's all right," sobbed Jane, as she began to cry again. "I really miss him, and I couldn't bear it if anything happened to him."

"Neither could I," said Amy. "I'm sorry but I've really got to go now. The lunch break is the only chance I've got to find you a cat."

Jane wiped her tears away with a tissue and handed Amy a piece of paper. "Don't forget to ask the owner to fill in this form. Star Pets can't use someone else's animal without their permission."

Amy tucked the form in her sleeve and set off toward the Primrose with Hilton and Plato. But she had only walked a few steps away from the movie set when a security guard dressed in black barred her way.

"You can't leave here in costume," he declared. "It might get damaged."

"But I've got to go home," said Amy. "There's something I need to get."

"It doesn't matter if there is," said the security guard. "Rules is rules. And the rules say no one in costume can leave the set. It would be more than my job's worth to let you go looking like that."

"All right," said Amy with a sigh. She turned and headed for the dressing rooms. But Hilton and Plato didn't.

"We'll go on ahead and organize a clan meeting," said Hilton.

"It'll save time," said Plato.

"Great," said Amy. She was the only human member of the group of animals that looked after Clamerkin Island. Hilton and Plato belonged too. The others were all cats, and she was hoping that one of them might be willing to help Jane.

The dressing-room tent was deserted, and Amy soon discovered why. "No one's allowed in here," said the lady in charge of the wardrobe as she shooed Amy out. "You must stay in your costume until filming is finished for the day."

"I can't," said Amy. "I've got to get something from home." But her arguments were no more effective here than they had been with the security guard.

Amy felt like screaming with

frustration. The first rule said she couldn't leave the set in her costume. The second said that she couldn't take it off. There was no way she could help Jane find a cat without breaking one of them. But which one would it be?

She waited until the wardrobe lady was busy eating a  sandwich. Then she slipped inside the tent, and found her normal clothes hanging on a hook labeled "Girl 5". She took them into one of the cubicles and changed as quickly as she could. Then she slipped quietly out of the tent again without being seen.

This time the security guard took no notice of her at all. As soon as she was past him, she broke into a run. The lunch break only lasted an hour – she couldn't afford to waste any more time.

CHAPTER SIX

The clan's almost-secret meeting place
was in the middle of the bushes at the
end of Amy's garden. Three of the cats
were already there when she arrived.
Willow, the Siamese from the post
office was sitting on the grass washing
her tail. On one side of her sat Einstein,
the white Persian who lived at the
school and on the other lay Bun, the

fat black and white cat from the bakery.

"Where's Isambard?" asked Amy.

"He promised he'd be here," said Hilton.

"And I am," puffed the tabby cat, as he ran into the clearing. "Sorry I'm late. The director wanted me for some close-ups."

Willow gave him a disapproving glance. "Everyone's obsessed with this filming. They're talking about nothing else at the post office."

"The filming is the reason we've called the meeting," said Amy. She explained about Cuddles and how Dallas had refused to hold another dog. "So she wants a cat instead, and I thought one of you might like to do it."

Isambard shook his head. "Count me out. I've already got a part." He paused and stuck his nose in the air, before he added grandly, "I am the cat on the pile of sacks."

"Don't rub it in," said Plato. "There's some of us who'd give their eye teeth to be in that movie."

"You haven't got any teeth," said Hilton. "You've only got a beak."

"We're wandering off the subject," said Amy. "Jane needs a lap cat this afternoon. Have we got any volunteers?"

"Me!" cried Willow, Einstein and Bun at the same time.

"You can't all do it," said Hilton. "Dallas only has one lap."

"I'd be best," Willow insisted. "Siamese cats have experience of important roles. My ancestors lived with royalty."

"But you're not fluffy," said Einstein. "All the best lap cats are fluffy like me."

Bun sighed and gazed at Amy with huge, sad eyes. "I don't think I'd better do it after all. I'm not elegant and I'm not fluffy. I'm just fat."

"That means you're cuddly," said Amy.

"Did someone call me?" cried a voice from deep in the bushes. The leaves rustled and shook. Then a small ball of brown and black fur hurtled into the clearing.

Amy jumped back in surprise. "Cuddles!" she cried. "Is that really you?" The new arrival looked very different from the lapdog that had run away that morning. His bow had disappeared.  His long, silky hair was full of tangles and his feet were covered with mud. But the biggest change of all was that he was happy.

The Yorkshire terrier opened his mouth in a doggy grin and wagged his tail as hard as he could. "Yes, it's me – the new me. The me who sniffs trees and rolls in mud."

"And the me who bites people," said Hilton. His voice was tinged with disapproval.

"Only the once," said Cuddles. "Just so I could escape. I'm not going to make a habit of it." He grinned again and asked, "What are you all doing?"

"We're deciding who's going to take your place in the movie," said Plato. "Dallas doesn't want another dog or a parrot. So it's got to be a cat."

"And we all want to do it," said Willow.

"Except me," purred Isambard.

"We'd better hurry up," said Amy. "If we don't decide soon which one of you it's going to be, Jane won't have time to get you ready."

Willow looked at her suspiciously. "What exactly does getting ready involve?"

"I know the answer to that," said Cuddles, bouncing up and down with enthusiasm. "You have to have a bath and…"

"Bath!" shrieked Willow. Her tail shot straight up in the air in alarm, and the hairs on it stuck out sideways like the bristles on a bottlebrush. "I'm not being in the movie if I have to have a bath."

"Neither am I," mewed Einstein. He wasn't very good at the bottlebrush trick. So he crouched low to the ground instead and backed away. "I don't do baths. They're WET!"

"Horribly wet," added Bun. "Baths
are some of the horriblest things in
the whole wide world. Just thinking of
them makes me feel hungry."

"That's not surprising," muttered
Isambard. "Thinking of anything
makes *you* feel hungry."

Amy's heart sank. The cats'

enthusiasm for being in the movie had completely disappeared and with it had gone her chance of helping Jane. "Isn't there anything good about being in a movie?" she asked Cuddles.

The Yorkshire terrier wrinkled his nose thoughtfully. "Not really. There's lots of waiting around and being brushed and being groomed."

Willow stuck her nose in the air and licked one of her paws. "I do my own grooming, thank you."

Cuddles ignored her and continued. "I suppose the treats are a plus. Jane gives them to me as a reward for doing what I'm told."

Bun pricked up his ears. "What sort of treats?"

"Biscuits, mainly," the dog replied. "Sometimes it's bacon-flavored dog treats, and sometimes it's little pieces of cheese. I love cheese."

"I love sardines," said Bun. "Does she ever give you those?"

Cuddles shook his head. "It wouldn't work if she did. I hate fish."

"I expect she'd give some to you," said Amy. "I can tell her they're your favorites."

"In that case, I'm willing to be the lap cat." Bun stood up and strode over to Amy. "I'll do anything for a sardine."

"Even have a *bath*," said Willow.

"With *water*," added Einstein.

Bun shuddered. But the thought of sardines gave him the confidence he needed. "Even that," he promised and jumped into Amy's arms.

CHAPTER SEVEN

Amy shifted Bun so he was balanced on her right arm with his head over her shoulder. Then she patted her leg with her free hand and called, "Come on, Cuddles. Time to go home."

"No," barked Cuddles. He backed away from her and took shelter under a nearby bush. "I want to stay here."

"Please come," begged Amy.

"No," barked Cuddles, even more firmly than before. "I'm tired of humans fussing over me."

"I like it," said Bun. "Fussing usually means food."

Willow strode over to the bush and peered under the branches. "I hope it doesn't rain tonight. You'll get very wet in here if it does."

"That's the trouble with not having a roof," said Isambard. "Wonderful things, roofs. You always get one if you live with a human."

"You get warm places to sleep as well," said Einstein. "It won't be warm under that bush in the middle of the night, and you'll be all alone because all of us will have gone home."

Cuddles crept out from under the branches. He didn't look quite as confident as he had before. "You're just trying to make me change my mind," he grumbled. "But I mean what I said. I'm not going back there – not for anything."

"Not even to make Jane happy?" said Amy.

Cuddles gave a huge sigh and hung his head low. "She'll be happier without me. She won't want me now – not after I've been so bad."

Amy popped Bun on the ground so her arms were free. Then she wrapped them around the Yorkshire terrier and gave him a huge hug. "Of course Jane wants you back. Last time I saw her she was crying because she misses you so much."

"Really?" said Cuddles.

"Absolutely truly," said Hilton. "I saw her too."

Cuddles grinned and wagged his tail. "In that case, what are we waiting for? Let's go back."

*

Amy set off down the cobbled street to the harbor with Bun purring happily in her arms. Cuddles trotted on one side of her and Hilton on the other. But Plato flew on ahead, eager to see what was happening on the movie set.

As they passed the bakery, Amy remembered the permission form in her pocket. So she went inside the shop to talk to Bun's human.

The baker was almost as fat as his cat. He had a round face, a round tummy and round glasses. He beamed when he saw who Amy was carrying. Then he spotted Cuddles and his eyes widened in alarm.

"Watch out!" he said as he pushed

Amy to one side. He grabbed a broom from behind the counter and brandished it like a weapon. Then he advanced on the bedraggled Yorkshire terrier, saying. "I don't want any fancy rats in here."

Hilton gave a warning growl and jumped between the baker and his intended victim. At the same time, Amy grabbed hold of the broom and shouted, "He's not a rat. He's a dog."

The baker stopped and put down the broom. He took off his glasses and wiped the floury fingermarks off the lenses with his apron. Then he popped them back on his nose and stared at Cuddles.

"So he is," he said. "But he does look a little strange with him being so small and so muddy."

"He belongs to the movie people," said Amy. Then she explained all about Cuddles's bad behavior and the lap pet crisis. "So can they use Bun?" she asked finally.

"Of course they can," said the baker. He gave a beaming smile and tickled the fat cat's ears. "Imagine my old Bun being a star. I'll have to make sure I get the DVD."

While he was signing the form, Amy noticed the clock on the wall. It was later than she'd expected. She needed to hurry – the lunch break was nearly over.

She ran the rest of the way down the hill, clutching Bun and his paperwork. Hilton and Cuddles raced beside her. The Yorkshire terrier was struggling to keep up. His legs were even shorter than Hilton's and he was so used to being carried around that he wasn't very fit.

"Are we almost there yet?" he puffed, as they reached the end of the road. Then they turned the corner and saw Jane. The sight of her gave Cuddles an extra burst of energy.

"I'm back," he yapped, as he bounded toward her.

"Cuddles!" cried Jane. She picked him up and hugged him. "You're a bad dog, but I love you."

"I love you, too," yapped Cuddles. He wiggled in closer to her and licked her nose.

Jane giggled. Then she held him out at arm's length and examined him carefully. "You're absolutely filthy."

"But he's very happy," said Amy.
"I think he's enjoyed behaving like
a dog."

"I think he has, too," said Jane.
"Maybe I should let him do that more
often." She turned to Amy and said,
"I can't thank you enough for finding
him." Then she spotted what Amy was

carrying and squealed with delight. "You've found me a cat as well."

Amy nodded and handed her the completed form. "His name is Bun. He lives at the bakery."

Jane tucked Cuddles under one arm and hugged Amy with the other one. "You really are a miracle worker, Amy. You've solved both my problems at once." She reached down and tickled Bun's ears. "I've never been so happy to see a cat in all my life. He's a little grubby, but I can soon fix that with a bath."

Amy felt the black cat tense, ready to run away. "Tell her about the sardines," he mewed. "I'm not getting wet if she doesn't have any."

Amy winked at him. Then she looked at Jane. "You'll find Bun is very well behaved," she said. "He'll do anything you want in return for a sardine."

"Then he's going to have lots of them," said Jane. She reached in her pocket, pulled out a collar and leash and popped it onto Cuddles. Then she put the dog down and gently took Bun from Amy. "Come along, my sweetie," she said. "You're going to be even fatter by the time I've finished with you."

Bun's purr was louder than Amy had ever heard it before. He snuggled contentedly against Jane's blouse. "I'm going to enjoy this," he said.

Amy glowed with pleasure as
she watched him. Everything had
turned out well. The filming was fun,
Cuddles was safe and Dallas had the
pet she needed.

Then she glanced at Plato sitting
on his cage and felt a twinge of guilt.
That was one problem she hadn't
solved. It looked as if the parrot's
dreams of stardom would never
come true.

CHAPTER EIGHT

Suddenly, Fran arrived, looking hot and frazzled. "There you are, Amy," she said with a sigh of exasperation. "I've been looking for you everywhere." She tapped her pen on the top of her clipboard and frowned at Amy's jeans. "What are you doing dressed like that? No one's supposed to get changed in the middle of filming."

"I know," said Amy. "But I had to go home for something, and I wasn't allowed to go in my costume."

"She got us a cat," said Jane, holding out Bun for her to see.

Fran's face softened. "I suppose that's all right then." She smiled at Amy and added, "You'd better get ready right away. You're in the next scene."

Amy was pleased when Fran went with her to the dressing rooms to explain the situation. The wardrobe lady tutted disapprovingly when she realized Amy had broken the rules. But she helped her struggle back into her long dress, bonnet and boots and checked that she looked exactly the same as she had earlier.

As soon as Amy was ready, she ran back to the set. "How's Bun doing?" asked Isambard as she passed his pile of sacks.

"I don't know," she whispered. She searched the faces of the crowd of people behind the cameras, but there was no sign of Jane.

Then the director shouted "Action!" so Amy had to push thoughts of Bun out of her mind and concentrate on what she was doing. This time she had to pretend to talk without making a sound. It was really hard not to giggle as she silently mouthed words to Veronica. She could only do it if she didn't look her friend in the eye.

Every time there was a gap in filming, she looked around again for Jane. But the animal trainer still wasn't anywhere to be seen. Amy felt her stomach knot with nerves. Had something gone wrong? Had Bun refused to have the bath after all and run away?

Eventually, Fran told all the extras to take a break while the director tried again to film the scene Cuddles had wrecked that morning. As Dallas Riba strode back onto the set, Amy wiggled as close as she could to the cameras to get a good view of the black cat's big moment. But she wasn't sure it was ever going to happen. Bun still hadn't turned up.

"Where's the cat?" asked Dallas.

"Where's the cat?" shouted the director.

The question rippled through the crowd of people watching. Then Jane finally appeared, carrying Bun on a velvet cushion.

At least, Amy assumed it was Bun. She had never seen the baker's cat look quite like that before. He was washed and brushed. His white paws were spotless and his gleaming fur was almost as fluffy as Einstein's.

As Jane carried Bun past her, Amy caught a distinct whiff of sardines. No wonder the fat cat looked so contented.

"He's divine," gushed Dallas as she took Bun in her arms. Then she wrinkled her nose. "But he does smell a little fishy."

"Don't worry," said Jane. "I can soon deal with that." She pulled a bottle of perfume from her pocket and sprayed some over Bun.

The black cat's eyes opened wide with astonishment, but he didn't move.

Dallas sniffed approvingly. Then she started her scene. Bun behaved perfectly. With his tummy so full of sardines, he was happy to lie still in her arms while the action went on around him.

"Cut," called the director, when Dallas had finished her lines. Then he turned to Jane and said, "That cat's a natural. You did well to find him."

"It wasn't me," she replied. She caught hold of Amy's hand and pulled her out of the crowd. "It was Amy."

The director smiled. "Then we have you to thank, young lady. I hope you're enjoying being in the movie."

Amy nodded. "It's fun," she said shyly. Then she plucked up all her courage, swallowed hard and added, "But it would be even better if you could do something for me."

The director took a step back in surprise. "That will depend what it is

you're after. Do you want a better part
or a line or two to say?"

"No," said Amy. She pointed to Plato
who was still sitting on top of his cage.
"It's my parrot. He wants to be – I
mean – I want him to be in the movie."

The director shook his head. "I'm sorry. That's not possible. The *Black Raven*'s not a pirate ship and only pirates had parrots."

But Amy wasn't willing to take no for an answer when success was so tantalizingly close. She smiled what she hoped was her sweetest smile and said, "I'm sure ordinary sailors must have had parrots, too. Otherwise it would have been too easy to spot the pirates."

"That's an interesting point of view," said the director, as he stroked his chin thoughtfully. "But I'm not sure you're right."

"I am," said Jane. "My great-great-grandfather was the captain of a ship

that looked just like the *Black Raven*.
He definitely wasn't a pirate, but we've
got a picture of him with a parrot on
his shoulder."

"That's very interesting," said the
director, stroking his chin thoughtfully.
"Perhaps our ship should have a
parrot after all – to make it look more
realistic."

Amy saw her chance and pushed
even harder. "Plato would be perfect,"
she insisted. "He'll look great on screen.
He's very colorful."

The director nodded. "I think you
might be right." Then he smiled at
Amy and added, "Your parrot's got
a part."

Plato was beside himself with

excitement when Amy told him the news.
"I'm going to be a star," he squawked,
as he flapped his wings in delight.

"But you've got to behave," Amy
warned.

"I will," the parrot promised.

For the rest of the week, Plato perched happily on Mr. Plimstone's shoulder and acted the part of the perfect sailor's parrot. He didn't nip the principal's ear. He didn't squawk "Pieces of eight." And he only winked at the cameras when no one else was looking.

The End

Amy Wild, Animal Talker

Collect all of Amy's fun
and fur-filled adventures!

The Secret Necklace

Amy is thrilled to discover she can talk to animals!
But making friends is harder than she thought...

The Musical Mouse

There's a singing mouse at Amy's school! Can Amy
find it a new home before the principal catches it?

The Mystery Cat

Amy has to track down the owners of a playful
orange cat who's lost his home...and his memory.

The Furry Detectives

Things have been going missing on the Island and
Amy suspects there's a thief at work.

The Great Sheep Race

Will Amy train the Island's sheep in time for her school fair's big fundraiser – a Great Sheep Race?

The Star-Struck Parrot

Amy gets to be an extra in a movie shot on the Island...but can she land Plato the parrot a part too?

The Lost Treasure

An ancient ring is discovered on the Island, sparking a hunt for buried treasure...and causing chaos.

The Vanishing Cat

When one of the animals in the clan goes missing, Amy faces her biggest mystery yet...